Princeton University

Charter and By-Laws of the Trustees

together with a statement concerning the original charter, and the rules of

order of the board

Princeton University

Charter and By-Laws of the Trustees
together with a statement concerning the original charter, and the rules of order of the board

ISBN/EAN: 9783337369712

Printed in Europe, USA, Canada, Australia, Japan

Cover: Foto ©Andreas Hilbeck / pixelio.de

More available books at **www.hansebooks.com**

The

Charter and By-Laws

of

The Trustees of

Princeton University

Together with

A Statement Concerning the Original Charter,

and

The Rules of Order of the Board.

Printed by order of the
Board of Trustees.
1899.

PRESS OF
JOHN C. RANKIN CO.
24 CORTLANDT ST.
NEW YORK

General Index

Statement

Concerning the Original Charter of Princeton University.

The first Charter of Princeton University passed the Great Seal of the Province of New Jersey on the 22d of October, A. D. 1746. This appears from facts hereinafter stated, viewed in connection with a Record in the office of the Secretary of State of the State of New Jersey, of which the following is the print of a certified copy.

Extracts from the Records of the Province of New Jersey.

A CHARTER TO INCORPORATE SUNDRY PERSONS TO FOUND A COLLEDGE PASS'D THE GREAT SEAL OF THIS PROVINCE OF NEW JERSEY, TESTED BY JOHN HAMILTON, ESQ., PRESIDENT OF HIS MAJESTY'S COUNCIL, AND COMMANDER IN CHIEF OF THE PROVINCE OF NEW JERSEY, THE 22d OCTOBER, 1746.

STATE OF NEW JERSEY, } ss.
DEPARTMENT OF STATE. }

I, Henry C. Kelsey, Secretary of State of the State of New Jersey, do hereby certify that the foregoing is a true copy of a certain record as the same is taken from and compared with the original record recorded in Book C 2 of Commissions, on page 137, and now remaining on file in my office.

IN TESTIMONY WHEREOF, I have hereunto set my hand and affixed my official seal, at Trenton, this twenty-fifth day of March, A. D. 1891.

(Signed) HENRY C. KELSEY,
Secretary of State.

The Charter thus mentioned has been lost—certainly for more than a century. Strange to say, no transcript of it was entered upon the Records of the Province, and no copy, so far as can be ascertained by the authorities of the University, is in existence. It was recently discovered, however, that an extended "Notice," published at Philadelphia, A. D. 1747, in two Philadelphia journals, contains what is manifestly a full abstract of the lost instrument. The papers containing this Notice are the *Pennsylvania Journal*, in its issues of August 13th, 27th, and September 10th, and the *Pennsylvania Gazette*, in its issues of August 13th and 27th. A copy of this document is given below.

It is manifest, from the date assigned in the Notice to the Charter mentioned therein, viz., October 22, 1746, that the instrument mentioned was the one whose passage of the Great Seal was recorded, as above set forth, in the Records of the Province of New Jersey. It will also appear, upon a comparison of the Notice with the Charter of the College of New Jersey, granted A. D. 1748, that the Charter mentioned in the former relates to the institution contemplated in the latter. The names of the corporators and the provisions of the two instruments are almost identical,* and the facts set forth in the Notice concerning the establishment of a College correspond with well-established facts in the history of what, for one hundred and fifty years, was known as the College of New Jersey. On February 13th, 1896, under legislative authority, the corporate name of the institution was changed from The Trustees of the College of New Jersey to The Trustees of Princeton University.

NOTICE.

THESE ARE TO GIVE NOTICE TO ALL CONCERNED

That by His Majesty's Royal Charter for erecting a College in New Jersey, for the instruction of youth in the learned Languages and in the liberal Arts and Sciences,

---

* The number of Trustees (original and elected) mentioned in the Notice was only *twelve*. All of these gentlemen, with the exception of the Rev. Messrs. Dickinson and Finley, were amongst the corporators mentioned in the Charter of 1748. Of the two gentlemen excepted it should be noted that the Rev. Mr. Dickinson died in 1747, before the granting of the second charter; and that the Rev. Mr. Finley was elected a Trustee in 1751. Dr. Finley held his office as Trustee until 1761, in which year he assumed the office of President of the Institution.

bearing date October 22nd, 1746, Messrs. William Smith, Peter Vanbrugh Livingston, William Peartree Smith, Gent., and Messrs. Johnathan Dickinson, John Pierson, Ebenezer Pemberton, and Aaron Burr, Ministers of the Gospel, are appointed Trustees of the said College; with full power to any four or more of them, to chuse five more Trustees to the exercise of equal power and authority in the said College, with themselves. By virtue of which power, the said Trustees, nominated in the Charter, have chosen the Rev. Messrs. Gilbert Tennant, William Tennant, Samuel Blair, Richard Treat, and Samuel Finley, as Trustees of the said College of New-Jersey : Which Trustees are by the said Charter, constituted a body corporate and politick, both in fact and name, with full power to act as such to all intents and purposes, and rendred capable of a perpetual succession to continue forever. By which Royal Charter, there is authority given to the major part of any seven or more of the said Trustees, and their successors conven'd for that purpose, to purchase, receive, and dispose of any possessions, tenements, goods and chattels, gifts, legacies, donations and bequests, rents,* profits, and annuities of any kind whatsoever, and to build any house or houses, as they shall think proper, for the use of the said College. And also by the said Charter is given to the major part of any seven or more of the said Trustees and their successors, full power to chuse, and at pleasure to displace, a President, Tutors, Professors, Treasurer, Clerk, Steward and Usher, with any other ministers and officers as are usual in any of the Universities or Colleges in the realm of Great Britain. And also by the said Charter, is given to the major part of any seven or more† of the said Trustees and their successors, full power to make any laws, acts and ordinances, for the government of the said College, as are not repugnant to the laws and statutes of the realm of Great Britain, nor to the laws of the Province of New Jersey; provided, that no person be debarred any of the privileges of the said College on account of any speculative principles of religion ; but those of every religious profession have equal privilege and advantage of education in the said College. And also by the said Charter, power is given to the major part of any seven of the said Trustees and their successors, by their President, or any other appointed by them, to give any such degrees as are given in any of the Universities or Colleges in the realm of Great Britain, to any such as they shall judge qualified for such degrees; and power to have and use a common seal to seal and confirm diplomas or certificates of such degrees, or for any other use which they shall think proper.

And these may further notify all concern'd, that the said Trustees have chosen the Rev. Mr. Johnathan Dickinson, President, whose superior abilities are well known ; and Mr. Caleb Smith, Tutor, of the said College ; and that the College is now actually opened, to be kept at Elizabeth-Town, till a building can be erected in a more central place of the said‡ province for the residence of the students ; that all who are qualified for it, may be immediately admitted to an academick education, and to such class and station in the College, as they are found upon examination to deserve ; and that the charge of the College to each student, will be Four Pounds a year New Jersey money, at Eight Shillings per ounce, and no more.

* As in Gazette; omitted in Journal.
† As in Journal; omitted in Gazette.
‡ As in Gazette; omitted in Journal.

Charter

Note.

The paragraphs that have been repealed are printed with STARS at the beginning of the lines. Single words, or clauses, that have been altered or repealed are printed in *italics*.

Charter

of the

College of New Jersey.*

[September 14th, 1748.]

GEORGE THE SECOND, by the grace of God, of Great Britain, France and Ireland, King, Defender of the Faith, etc., to all to whom these presents shall come, greeting—

WHEREAS sundry of our loving subjects, well-disposed and public-spirited persons, have lately, by their humble petition, presented to our trusty and well-beloved Jonathan Belcher, Esquire, Governor and Commander in Chief of our province of New Jersey in America, represented the great necessity of coming into some method for encouraging and promoting a learned education of our youth in New Jersey, and have expressed their earnest desire that a college may be erected in our said province of New Jersey in America, for the benefit of the inhabitants of the said province and others, wherein youth may be instructed in the learned languages, and in the liberal arts and sciences. AND WHEREAS by the fundamental concessions made at the first settlement of New Jersey by the Lord Berkley and Sir George Carteret, then proprietors thereof, and granted under their hands and the seal of the said province, bearing date the tenth day of February, in the year of our Lord one thousand six hundred and sixty-four, it was, among other things, conceded and agreed, that no freeman, within the said province of

Preamble

* By authority of the General Act of the Legislature approved April 12th, 1894, page 38, and by action of the Board of Trustees taken February 13th, 1896, page 40, the corporate title of "THE TRUSTEES OF THE COLLEGE OF NEW JERSEY" was on October 22d, 1896, changed to "THE TRUSTEES OF PRINCETON UNIVERSITY."

New Jersey, should at any time be molested, punished, disquieted,
or called in question, for any difference in opinion or practice in
matters of religious concernment, who do not actually disturb the
civil peace of the said province : but that all and every such person
or persons might, from time to time, and at all times thereafter,
freely and fully have and enjoy his and their judgments and con-
sciences, in matters of religion, throughout the said province, they
behaving themselves peaceably and quietly and not using this
liberty to licentiousness, nor to the civil injury or outward dis-
turbance of others, as by the said concessions on record in the
Secretary's office of New Jersey, at Perth Amboy, in lib. 3, folio
66, etc., may appear. WHEREFORE and for that the said petitioners
have also expressed their earnest desire that those of every religious
denomination may have free and equal liberty and advantages of
education in the said college, any different sentiments in religion
notwithstanding. WE being willing to grant the reasonable requests
and prayers of all our loving subjects, and to promote a liberal
and learned education among them—

KNOW YE THEREFORE, that we, considering the premises, and
being willing for the future that the best means of education be
established in our said province of New Jersey, for the benefit and
advantage of the inhabitants of our said province and others, do,
of our special grace, certain knowledge and mere motion, by these
presents, will, ordain, grant, and constitute, that there be a college
erected in our said province of New Jersey, for the education of
youth in the learned languages and in the liberal arts and sciences ; *
and that the trustees of the said college and their successors for
ever, may and shall be one body corporate and politic, in deed,
action and name, and shall be called, and named and distinguished,
by the name of THE TRUSTEES OF THE COLLEGE OF NEW JERSEY †
and further, we have willed, given, granted, constituted, and appointed, and by this our present charter, of our special grace,
certain knowledge, and mere motion, we do, for us, our heirs and
successors, will, give, grant, constitute, and ordain, that there shall,
in the said college, from henceforth for ever, be a body politic,

College founded

Trustees a Corporation

Corporate name

* Extended by the Act of March 11th, 1864.
† See foot-note * page 11.

consisting of Trustees of the said College of New Jersey. And, for
the more full and perfect erection of the said corporation and body
politic consisting of Trustees of the College of New Jersey, we, of
our special grace, certain knowledge, and mere motion, do, by
these presents, for us, our heirs and successors, create, make, ordain,
constitute, nominate, and appoint, the Governor and Commander
in Chief of our said province of New Jersey, for the time being, and
also our trusty and well-beloved John Reading, James Hude,
Andrew Johnston, Thomas Leonard, John Kinsey, Edward Shippen
and William Smith, Esquires, Peter Van-Brugh Livingston,
William Peartree Smith, and Samuel Hazard, gentlemen, John
Pierson, Ebenezer Pemberton, Joseph Lamb, Gilbert Tennent,
William Tennent, Richard Treat, Samuel Blair, David Cowell, Aaron
Burr, Timothy Jones, Thomas Arthur, and Jacob Green, ministers '
of the gospel, to be Trustees of the said College of New Jersey.

* That the said Trustees do, at their first meeting, after the receipt
* of these presents, and before they proceed to any business, take
* the oath appointed to be taken by an act, passed in the first year
* of the reign of the late King George the First, entitled, "An act
* for the further security of his Majesty's person and government,
* and the succession of the crown in the heirs of the late princess
* Sophia, being protestants, and for extinguishing the hopes of
* the pretended prince of Wales, and his open and secret abettors ";
* as also that they make and subscribe the declarations mentioned
* in an act of parliament, made in the twenty-fifth year of the reign
* of King Charles the Second, entitled, "An act for preventing
* dangers which may happen from popish recusants "; and likewise
* take an oath for faithfully executing the office or trust reposed in
* them, the said oaths to be administered to them by three of his
* Majesty's justices of the peace, *quorum unus* ; and when any
* new member or officer of this corporation is chosen, they are to
* take and subscribe the aforementioned oaths and declarations
* before their admission into their trusts or offices, the same to be ad-
* ministered to them in the presence of the Trustees, by such person
* as they shall appoint for that service.*

Marginal notes: Charter perpetual / Names of corporators / Oaths to be taken by Trustees / By whom oaths are to be administered

The entire clause relative to oaths repealed and supplied by Act of March 13th, 1780; and further
amended by Act of March 29th, 1866.

Notice of meeting of Trustees

That no meeting of the Trustees shall be valid or legal for doing any business whatsoever, unless the clerk has duly and legally notified each and every member of the corporation of such meeting ; and that before the entering on any business, the clerk shall certify such notification under his hand, to the Board of Trustees.

To fill vacancies

Number of Trustees

That the said Trustees have full power and authority or any *thirteen*† or greater number of them, to elect, nominate, and appoint, and associate unto them, any number of persons as Trustees upon any vacancy, so that the whole number of Trustees exceed not *twenty-three*‡ whereof the President of the said college for the time being, to be chosen as hereafter mentioned, to be one, and twelve of the said Trustees to be always such persons as are in-

Residence

habitants of our said province of New Jersey. And we do further, of our special grace, certain knowledge, and mere motion, for us,

Perpetual succession

our heirs and successors, will, give, grant, and appoint, that the said Trustees and their successors shall, for ever hereafter, be in deed, fact and name, a body corporate and politic ; and that they, the said body corporate and politic, shall be known and distinguished in all deeds, grants, bargains, sales, writings, evidences, muniments, or otherwise howsoever, and in all courts for ever hereafter, plead and be impleaded, by the name of THE TRUSTEES OF THE COLLEGE OF NEW JERSEY.**

Property

And that they, the said corporation, by the name aforesaid, shall be able, and in law capable, for the use of the said college, to have, get, acquire, purchase, receive and possess lands, tenements, hereditaments, jurisdictions, and franchises, for themselves and their successors, in fee simple or otherwise howsoever ; and to purchase, receive or build, any house or houses, or any other buildings, as they shall think needful or convenient for the use of the said College of New Jersey, and in such place or places in New Jersey, as they, the said Trustees shall agree upon, and also to receive and dispose of any goods, chattels, and other things of what nature soever,

---

† Altered to *nine*, provided that the Governor of the State, or the President of the College, or the senior Trustee, be one of the nine ; by the Act of Nov. 2d, 1781.

‡ Altered to *twenty-seven* by the Act of April 6th, 1868.

* * See foot-note * page 11.

for the use aforesaid : and also to have, accept and receive, any
rents, profits, annuities, gifts, legacies, donations and bequests, of   Limitation
any kind whatsoever, for the use aforesaid, so, nevertheless, that   of value of
                                                                          estate
the yearly clear value of the premises do not exceed the sum of
two thousand pounds sterling.† And therewith or otherwise to
support and pay, (as the said Trustees and their successors, or the
major part of such of them as [according to the provision herein
afterwards] are regularly convened for that purpose, shall agree and
see cause,) the President, tutors, and other officers or ministers of   Salaries
the said college, their respective annual salaries or allowances, and
all such other necessary and contingent charges as from time to
time shall arise and accrue, relating to the said college ; and also
to grant, bargain, sell, let, set or assign, lands, tenements or hereditaments, goods or chattels, contract or do all other things whatso-   Contracts
ever, by the name aforesaid, and for the use aforesaid, in as full
and ample manner, to all intents and purposes, as any natural person or other body politic or corporate is able to do, by the laws of
our realm of Great Britain, or of our said province of New Jersey.

And of our further grace, certain knowledge and mere motion,   Who to
to the intent that our said corporation and body politic may   preside
answer the end of their erection and constitution, and may have
perpetual succession and continue forever, WE do for us, our heirs
and successors, hereby will, give, and grant, unto the said Trustees
of the College of New Jersey, and to their successors forever, that
when any *thirteen* * of the said Trustees, or of their successors, are
convened and met together as aforesaid, for the service of the said
college, the Governor and Commander in Chief of our said province
of New Jersey, and in his absence, the President of the said college,
and in the absence of the said Governor and President, the eldest
Trustee present at such meeting, from time to time, shall be President of the said Trustees in all their meetings : and at any time or

---

† Altered to *the value of twenty thousand bushels of wheat* by the Act of March 13, 1780; to
twenty thousand dollars, May 27, 1799; to *one hundred thousand dollars*, March 11, 1864; to *five
hundred thousand dollars*, by resolution of the Trustees adopted June 17, 1889, and filed in the office
of the Secretary of State, June 26, 1889, in accordance with the provisions of the Act of March
27, 1889.

* See foot-note, ‡, p. 14.

times such *thirteen* * Trustees convened and met as aforesaid, shall be capable to act as fully and amply, to all intents and purposes as if all the Trustees of the said college were personally present, provided always, that a majority of the said *thirteen* * Trustees be of the said province of New Jersey, except after regular notice they fail of coming, in which case those that are present are hereby em-

powered to act, the different place of their abode notwithstanding, and all affairs and actions whatsoever, under the care of the said Trustees, shall be determined by the majority or greater number of those *thirteen* *, so convened and met together, the President whereof shall have no more than a single vote.

And we do for us, our heirs and successors, hereby will, give, and grant, full power and authority, to any six or more of the said Trustees, to call meetings of the said Trustees, from time to time, and to order notice to the said Trustees of the times and places of meeting for the service aforesaid.

And also we do hereby for us, our heirs and successors, will give, and grant, to the said Trustees of the College of New Jersey, and to their successors for ever, that the said Trustees do elect, nominate and appoint such a qualified person as they, or the major part of any *thirteen* * of them convened for that purpose as above directed, shall think fit, to be the President of the said college, and to have the immediate care of the education and government of such students as shall be sent to, and admitted into the said college for instruction and education ; and also that the said Trustees do

elect, nominate and appoint so many tutors and professors, to assist the President of the said college, in the education and government of the students belonging to it, as they, the said Trustees, or their successors, or the major part of any *thirteen* * of them, which shall convene for that purpose as above directed, shall, from time to time, and at any time hereafter, think needful and serviceable to the interests of the said college ; and also, that the said Trustees and their successors, or the major part of any *thirteen* * of them, which shall convene for that purpose, as above directed, shall at

any time displace and discharge from the service of the said college

---

* See foot-note, †, p. 14.

such President, tutors and professors, and to elect others in their room and stead ; and also, that the said Trustees or their successors, or the major part of any *thirteen*[*] of them, which shall convene for that purpose, as above directed, do from time to time, as occasion shall require, elect, constitute, and appoint a treasurer, a clerk, an usher, and a steward, for the said college, and appoint to them, and each of them, their respective business and trusts, and displace and discharge from the service of the said college such treasurer, clerk, usher, or steward, and to elect others in their room and stead ; which President, tutors, professors, treasurer, clerk, usher, and steward, so elected and appointed, we do for us, our heirs and successors, by these presents constitute and establish in their several offices, and do give them, and every of them, full power and authority to exercise the same in the said College of New Jersey, according to the direction, and during the pleasure of the said Trustees, as fully and freely as any other, the like officers in our universities or any of our colleges, in our realm of Great Britain, lawfully may and ought to do.

And also that the said Trustees, and their successors, or the major part of any *thirteen*[*] of them, which shall convene for that purpose as above directed, as often as one or more of the said Trustees shall happen to die, or by removal or otherwise shall become unfit or uncapable, according to their judgment, to serve the interest of the said college, do, as soon as conveniently may be after the death, removal or such unfitness or incapacity of such Trustee or Trustees to serve the interest of the said college, elect and appoint such other Trustee or Trustees as shall supply the place of him or them so dying, or otherwise becoming unfit or uncapable to serve the interest of the said college ; and every Trustee so elected and appointed shall, by virtue of these presents, and of such election, and appointment, be vested with all the power and privileges which any of the other Trustees of the said college are hereby invested with.

And we do further, of our special grace, certain knowledge and mere motion, will, give and grant, and by these presents do,

Other officers

Power of officers

Election of Trustees

Laws for the government of the college

---

[*] See foot-note, 2, p. 14.

for us, our heirs and successors, will, give and grant, unto the said Trustees of the College of New Jersey, that they and their successors, or the major part of any *thirteen** of them, which shall convene for that purpose as above directed, may make, and they are hereby fully empowered from time to time, freely and lawfully to make and establish such ordinances, orders and laws, as may tend to the good and wholesome government of the said college, and all the students and the several officers and ministers thereof, and to the public benefit of the same, not repugnant to the laws and statutes of our realm of Great Britain, or of this our province of New Jersey, and not excluding any person of any religious denomination whatsoever from free and equal liberty and advantage of education, or from any of the liberties, privileges, or immunities of the said college, on account of his or their being of a religious profession different from the said Trustees of the said college; and such ordinances, orders, and laws, which shall be so as aforesaid made, we do, by these presents, for us, our heirs and successors, ratify, allow of, and confirm, as good and effectual, to oblige and bind all the said students and the several officers and ministers of the said college; and we do hereby authorize and empower the said Trustees of the college, and the President, tutors, and professors, by them elected and appointed, to put such ordinances and laws in execution, to all proper intents and purposes.

Degrees

And we do further, of our especial grace, certain knowledge, and mere motion, will, give, and grant, unto the said Trustees of the College of New Jersey, that, for the encouragement of learning and animating the students of the said college to diligence, industry, and a laudable progress in literature, that they and their successors, or the major part of any *thirteen** of them, convened for that purpose as above directed, do, by the President of the said college for the time being, or by any other deputed by them, give and grant any such degree and degrees to any of the students of the said college, or to any others by them thought worthy thereof, as are usually granted in either of our universities or any other

* See foot-note, 4, p. 14.

college in our realm of Great Britain† ; and that they do sign and seal diplomas or certificates of such graduations, to be kept by the graduates as perpetual memorials or testimonials thereof.

And further, of our especial grace, certain knowledge, and more motion, we do, by these presents, for us, our heirs and successors, give and grant unto the said Trustees of the College of New Jersey and to their successors, that they and their successors shall have a common Seal, under which they may pass all diplomas, certificates of degrees, and all other the affairs and business of and concerning the said corporation, or of and concerning the said College of New Jersey, which shall be engraven in such form and with such inscription as shall be devised by the said Trustees of the said college, or the major part of any *thirteen** of them, convened for the service of the said college as above directed.

And we do further, for us, our heirs and successors, give and grant unto the said Trustees of the College of New Jersey and their successors, or the major part of any *thirteen** of them, convened for the service of the college as above directed, full power and authority from time to time, to nominate and appoint all other inferior officers and ministers, which they shall think to be convenient and necessary for the use of the college, not herein particularly named or mentioned, and which are accustomary in our universities, or in any of our colleges in our realm of Great Britain, which officers or ministers we do hereby empower to execute their offices or trusts as fully and freely as any other the like officers or ministers, in and of our universities or any other college in our realm of Great Britain, lawfully may or ought to do.

And lastly, our express will and pleasure is, and we do by these presents for us, our heirs and successors, give and grant unto the said Trustees of the College of New Jersey, and to their successors for ever, that these our letters patent, or the enrolment thereof, shall be good and effectual in the law, to all intents and purposes, against us, our heirs and successors, without any other license, grant, or confirmation from us, our heirs and successors,

(margin notes: Diplomas, Seal, Inferior officers)

---

* See foot-note, ?, p. 11.
† Extended by the Act of March 29th, 1866.

hereafter by the said Trustees to be had or obtained ; notwithstanding the not reciting or misrecital, or not naming or misnaming of
the aforesaid offices, franchises, privileges, immunities, or other
the premises, or any of them : and notwithstanding a writ of *ad
quod damnum* hath not issued forth to inquire of the premises or
any of them, before the ensealing hereof ; any statute, act, ordi-
nance or provision, or any other matter or thing to the contrary
notwithstanding ; to have, hold, and enjoy, all and singular the
privileges, advantages, liberties, immunities, and all other the
premises herein and hereby granted and given, or which are
meant, mentioned, or intended to be herein and hereby given and
granted, unto them the said Trustees of the said College of New
Jersey, and to their successors for ever.

IN TESTIMONY whereof we have caused these our letters to be
made patent, and the Great Seal of our said province of New Jersey
to be hereunto affixed. WITNESS our trusty and well-beloved
JONATHAN BELCHER, Esquire, Governor and Commander in Chief
of our said province of New Jersey, this fourteenth day of September, in the twenty-second year of our reign, and in the year of
our Lord, one thousand seven hundred and forty-eight.

 I have perused and considered the written Charter of
incorporation, and find nothing contained therein inconsistent with his Majesty's interest or the honor of
the Crown.

    (Signed)   J. WARRELL, *Att. Gen'l.*

September the 13th, 1748.—This Charter, having been read in
Council, was consented to and approved of.

    (Signed)   CHA. READ, *Cl. Con.*

Let the Great Seal of the Province of New Jersey be affixed to
this Charter.

    (Signed)   J. BELCHER.

To the Secretary of the Province of New Jersey.

Laws of New Jersey

Establishing and Amending

The Charter

and otherwise relating to

The University

Index of Amendments

Laws of New Jersey

Establishing and Amending the Charter.

I.

** AN ACT for amending and establishing the Charter of the College of
* New Jersey.* [March 13th, 1780.]

* WHEREAS the Trustees of the College of New Jersey,† by Preamble
* their humble petition presented to the legislature, have set forth,
* that his majesty George the Second, King of Great Britain, by
* his royal charter of incorporation, under the great seal of the
* then province of New Jersey, and bearing date the fourteenth
* day of September, in the twenty-second year of his reign, was
* pleased to incorporate sundry persons, to the number of twenty-
* three, by the name and style of "The Trustees of the College of
* New Jersey"; and did thereby among other things, grant unto
* them power and authority to erect, endow and govern a college
* for the instruction of youth in the learned languages, and liberal
* arts and sciences, as by the said charter of incorporation, recorded
* in the Secretary's office at Perth Amboy, in book C, number 2,
* pages 196 to 204, inclusive, reference being thereunto had, may
* more fully and at large appear: AND WHEREAS the said Trustees,
* by their said petition, have prayed that the same charter may be
* established and confirmed under the present happy constitution,
* with certain alterations and amendments, in their said petition
* mentioned and described: AND WHEREAS all wise legislatures
* have deemed the education of youth to be of the utmost impor-
* tance to the prosperity of a State, and have taken institutions for
* that purpose established under their patronage and protection:
* AND WHEREAS the said College of New Jersey hath been found
* greatly useful in diffusing as well the principles of political
* liberty, as of religion and literature, and many have thereby been

---

* Repealed, and supplied by the Act of May 27th, 1799.
† See foot-note * page 11.

* fitted to fill distinguished places, both in the civil and ecclesi-
* astical departments of this and of the other United States, with
* advantage to the community, and honor and reputation to them-
* selves : therefore, for granting the prayer of the petition of the
* said Trustees, so far forth as the same appears just and reason-
* able—

Charter, with
exceptions,
confirmed

* 1. BE IT ENACTED BY THE COUNCIL AND GENERAL ASSEMBLY
* OF THIS STATE, AND IT IS HEREBY ENACTED BY THE AUTHORITY OF
* THE SAME, That the said charter, with all and singular the advan-
* tages, privileges and immunities, and all other matters and things
* therein contained, such clauses and parts only excepted as are by
* this act repealed, altered or amended, is hereby established and
* confirmed ; and shall for ever hereafter be held and esteemed as
* good and effectual in law, to all intents, constructions, and pur-
* poses, as the same hath heretofore been held and esteemed, and
* as if the same were herein particularly recited ; any misuser, non-
* user, or any other default heretofore committed or suffered not-
* withstanding.

Trustees, their
privileges, etc.

* 2. AND BE IT ENACTED BY THE AUTHORITY AFORESAID, That
* the said Trustees of the College of New Jersey, and their suc-
* cessors, shall and may forever hereafter have, hold and enjoy, all
* and singular the advantages, privileges and immunities, granted
* in the said charter, and hereby confirmed unto them and their suc-
* cessors, in as full, ample and beneficial a manner, as if the same
* were given and granted to them by a law of this State, and as if
* every of the said advantages, privileges and immunities, were in
* the said law particularly enumerated and specified ; any law,
* usage or custom, relating to charters, notwithstanding.

Clause in
charter
respecting
oaths, repealed

* 3. AND BE IT ENACTED BY THE AUTHORITY AFORESAID, That
* the clause in the said charter directing and requiring the said
* Trustees, and each of them, and every officer of the said corpora-
* tion by them appointed, to take the oath of allegiance to the king
* of Great Britain and to make and subscribe the declaration as
* established by act of parliament under the former government,
* be and it hereby is repealed, discontinued, annulled and made

* Repealed and supplied by the Act of May 27th, 1799.

* void ; and in lieu thereof, such of the said Trustees or officers as
* are inhabitants of this State, and each of them, shall, at the next
* meeting of the said corporation after the passing of this act, or
* before they proceed further to execute their respective trusts and
* offices, take and subscribe the oaths or affirmations of allegiance
* and adjuration, as appointed and set forth in an act of the Coun-
* cil and General Assembly entitled, "An act for the security of
* the government of New Jersey," made and passed the nineteenth
* day of September, in the year of our Lord one thousand seven
* hundred and seventy-six, to be administered by any one justice
* of the peace of this State ; and such of them as are inhabitants of
* any other of the United States shall take and subscribe the oath or
* affirmation of adjuration in manner as aforesaid, and shall also
* produce a certificate from some one justice of the peace of the State
* to which they may respectively belong, setting forth that they
* have taken the oath or affirmation of allegiance to the said State ;
* and when any new member or officer of the said corporation shall
* be chosen, he shall take and subscribe the before mentioned oaths
* or affirmations, or take and subscribe the oath or affirmation of
* abjuration, and produce the certificate as aforesaid, before he is
* admitted to exercise his trust or office ; the said oaths or affirma-
* tions to be administered, in presence of the said Trustees, by the
* President of the said corporation for the time being.

Oaths to be taken by trustees

By whom oaths to be administered

* 4. AND BE IT FURTHER ENACTED BY THE AUTHORITY AFORE-
* SAID, That the said Trustees, and their successors, shall and may
* hold and enjoy any estate whatsoever, the clear yearly value
* whereof shall not exceed the value of twenty thousand bushels
* of wheat ; † any article or clause in the said charter to the con-
* trary notwithstanding.

Limitation of estate

* Passed at Trenton, March 13th, 1780.

---

* Repealed and supplied by the Act of May 27th, 1799.
† See foot-note, p. 15.

II.

* A SUPPLEMENTAL ACT to an Act entitled, "An Act for amending
* and establishing the Charter of the College of New Jersey." [November
* 2d, 1781.]

Preamble

    * "WHEREAS the Trustees of the College of New Jersey, by
* their petition to the legislature, have represented that, by their
* charter of incorporation, the number of thirteen Trustees is neces-
* sary to constitute a quorum for the transaction of all business
* relating to the said institution, to the great injury of their trust,
* by reason of the non attendance of many of their members who
* live at a distance ; and have prayed that the said quorum may
* be lessened ; and have also set forth that, notwithstanding the
* laws heretofore made and provided, divers soldiers of the troops
* and militia of these United States are often billeted and quartered
* in the buildings and their appurtenances provided for the recep-
* tion, convenience, and improvement of the students belonging to
* the said institution, to the great injury and destruction thereof ;
* and as it is thought reasonable, in order to promote the ends of
* so valuable and important an institution, to grant the prayer of
* the petitioners—

Nine to form
a quorum

    * 1. BE IT THEREFORE ENACTED BY THE COUNCIL AND GENERAL
* ASSEMBLY OF THIS STATE, AND IT IS HEREBY ENACTED BY THE
* AUTHORITY OF THE SAME, That from and after the passage of this
* act, it shall and may be lawful for any nine of the said Trustees,
* or a greater number of them, to convene and meet together ; and
* being so convened and met together, to form a board of the cor-
* poration instituted by the said charter, and be in all things a
* sufficient quorum for the doing, performing, and transacting all
* and every the duties and business of their said trust, to all intents
* and purposes whatever, as effectually as if thirteen of the said
* Trustees had so met and convened together for the purposes afore
* said, and shall, for and during the continuance of this act, be
* taken and considered as a full quorum of the said Trustees, in as

---

    * This Act, made perpetual by the Act of November 20th, 1786, was repealed, and the first
section supplied by the Act of May 27th, 1799.

* full and ample manner, and with the like powers, authorities,
* and interests as are given to and vested in thirteen of the said
* Trustees, in and by their said charter of incorporation, and shall
* be under the same directions, conditions, restrictions, provisos,
* and limitations, as to the benefit, conveniency and meetings of
* the said Trustees, as are contained in the said charter with respect
* to the quorum of thirteen Trustees aforesaid ; PROVIDED ALWAYS,
* that the Governor of this State for the time being, or in case of   Quorum, how constituted
* his death or absence, the President of the said college for the
* time being, and in case of the death or absence of both the said
* Governor and President, then the eldest Trustee of the said col-
* lege, shall always be one of the said nine Trustees, so at any
* time constituting a quorum as aforesaid.

* 2. AND BE IT ENACTED BY THE AUTHORITY AFORESAID, That   Troops not to be quartered in the college
* from and after the passing hereof, if any magistrate, military
* officer, quartermaster, or any other person whatever, shall
* billet, quarter, or place in, or cause to be billeted, quartered, or
* placed in the said college or the steward's house adjoining
* thereto, any officer, soldier, or other person belonging to or
* following the troops or militia of these United States, or either of
* them, without the consent of the said Trustees, or of some person
* or persons duly authorized by them, every such person so offend-
* ing shall forfeit, to and for the use of the said Trustees and their   Penalty
* successors, the sum of twenty shillings for every such officer,
* soldier, or other person so billeted, quartered, or placed in the
* said buildings, and that for each and every day such officer,
* soldier, or other person aforesaid, shall continue therein, the
* same to be recovered by the said Trustees, or their lawful attorney
* from the person so offending, together with the damages sus-
* tained and costs of suit, by action of debt in any court where the
* same may be cognizable.

* 3. AND BE IT ENACTED BY THE AUTHORITY AFORESAID, That   Limitation
* this act, and every clause and article therein contained, shall
* continue and be in force for the term of five years, and from

* Repealed by Act of May 27th, 1799.

* thence to the end of the next sitting of the General Assembly
* and no longer.
* Passed at Trenton, November 2d, 1781.

III.

* AN ACT to continue an act entitled, "A supplemental act to an act
* entitled, an act for amending and establishing the Charter of the College of
* New Jersey." [November 20th, 1786.]

Preamble

* WHEREAS the act entitled, "A supplemental act to an act
* entitled, an act for amending and establishing the charter of the
* College of New Jersey," passed at Trenton, the second day of
* November, one thousand seven hundred and eighty-one, will
* expire at the end of the next sitting of the General Assembly
* and it being represented that important and valuable purposes
* will be answered to that institution by a continuance of that act
* therefore—

Enacting
clause

* BE IT ENACTED BY THE COUNCIL AND GENERAL ASSEMBLY
* OF THIS STATE, AND IT IS HEREBY ENACTED BY THE AUTHORITY
* OF THE SAME, That the said recited act and every article and
* clause therein contained, except that part which limits the con-
* tinuation thereof, be and the same is hereby declared to be
* continued in full force, anything in the said act to the contrary
* notwithstanding.

* Passed at Trenton, November 20th, 1786.

IV.

AN ACT concerning the College of New Jersey. [February 19th, 1796.]

Preamble

WHEREAS it is the duty of a free and enlightened people to
patronize and promote the interest of science and literature, as the
surest basis of their liberty, property and prosperity: AND
WHEREAS it has been represented to the legislature, that the
College of New Jersey has suffered great injury during the late
war, in its buildings, library and philosophical apparatus, and that
its funds, in consequence of the devastations and calamities of the

---

* Repealed by Act of May 27th, 1799.

war, have been so impaired and diminished as to render it impracticable for the Trustees of the college to defray the expenses necessarily incident to the business and good management of the institution without some legislative aid, and it appearing to the legislature that a portion of the public money may be wisely and usefully appropriated to the aid and relief of the said college; therefore—

1. BE IT ENACTED BY THE COUNCIL AND GENERAL ASSEMBLY OF THIS STATE, AND IT IS HEREBY ENACTED BY THE AUTHORITY OF THE SAME, That from and after the passing of this act, there shall be paid by the treasurer of this State, for three years successively, the sum of six hundred pounds, in quarter-yearly payments, to the Trustees of the College of New Jersey, or their order; which sum shall be paid out of the interest on the loan-office money now in the treasury, or now due, or which hereafter may arise or become due on the loan-office money now in circulation; and the money so to be paid to the said Trustees, or their order, shall by them be laid out and appropriated to and for the repairs of the buildings of the college, its library, orrery, and philosophical apparatus. *Appropriation to college*

2. AND BE IT FURTHER ENACTED, That the receipt of the said Trustees, or their order, for so much money as may be received by them by virtue of this act, shall be a sufficient voucher for the treasurer of this State in the settlement of his accounts with the State. *Vouchers*

Passed at Trenton, February 19th, 1796.

V.

AN ACT relative to the College of New Jersey. [May 27th, 1799.]

WHEREAS, it appears that George the Second, King of Great Britain, by his charter of incorporation, bearing date the fourteenth day of September, in the year of our Lord one thousand seven hundred and forty-eight, did incorporate sundry persons, to the number of *twenty-three*,* by the name of "The Trustees of the College of New Jersey"; and did thereby, among other things, grant unto them power and authority to erect, endow and govern a col- *Preamble*

* See foot-note, †, p. 14.

lege, for the instruction of youth in the learned languages and liberal arts and sciences, as by the said charter of incorporation, recorded in the secretary's office in Book C, number 2, pages 196 to 204, inclusive, reference being thereunto had, may more fully appear; and whereas it is proper that the said charter, with certain alterations and amendments, should be established and confirmed under the present government; therefore—

Charter with exceptions, confirmed

1. BE IT ENACTED BY THE COUNCIL AND GENERAL ASSEMBLY OF THIS STATE, AND IT IS HEREBY ENACTED BY THE AUTHORITY OF THE SAME, That the said charter, with the advantages, privileges and immunities, and all other matters and things therein contained, such clauses and parts only excepted as are by this act repealed, altered, or amended, is hereby established and confirmed: and shall for ever hereafter be held and esteemed as good and effectual in law, to all intents, constructions and purposes, as the same hath heretofore been held and esteemed, and as if the same were herein particularly recited, any misuser, nonuser, or other default heretofore committed or suffered notwithstanding.

Trustees, their privileges

2. AND BE IT ENACTED, That the said Trustees of the College of New Jersey, and their successors, shall and may have, hold and enjoy, all the advantages, privileges, and immunities granted in the said charter, and hereby confirmed unto them and their successors, in as full, ample, and beneficial a manner as if the same were given and granted by a law of this State, and as if the said advantages, privileges and immunities were, in the said law, particularly specified and enumerated, any law, usage, or custom relating to charters notwithstanding.

Clause respecting oaths annulled

3. AND BE IT ENACTED, That the clause in the said charter, requiring every Trustee and officer of the said corporation to take and subscribe the oaths and declarations established by certain statutes of Great Britain, be and it hereby is revoked and annulled.

Oaths to be taken by resident Trustees and officers

* 4. AND BE IT ENACTED, That if any person, being an * inhabitant of this State, shall be elected a Trustee or officer of * the corporation, he shall, before he enters upon the duties of his * office, take and subscribe the oath to support the Constitution of

---

* Repealed and supplied by Act of March 29th, 1866.

* the United States and the oath of allegiance to this State pre-
* scribed by law, which oath any member of the said corporation
* is hereby authorized to administer; and if any person being an
* inhabitant of any other of the United States, shall be elected a
* Trustee or officer of the said corporation, he shall, before he enters
* upon the duties of his office, produce a certificate from some
* justice of the peace of the State in which he resides, setting forth,
* that he hath taken the oath to support the Constitution of the
* United States, and the oath of allegiance to the said State; *and*
* *further*, that it shall be lawful for any member of the said cor-
* poration to administer the oath of office to the person so elected.

By whom to be administered

Oaths to be taken by non-resident officers

5. AND WHEREAS the said corporation have represented that,
by their charter, thirteen members are requisite to constitute a
quorum, to the great injury of the institution and their trust, by
reason of the non-attendance of members who live at a distance, and
have prayed that the said quorum may be lessened: BE IT THERE-
FORE ENACTED, That any nine or more of the Trustees of the said
college, when duly convened, shall constitute a quorum, and be
competent to perform and execute all the duties, business, matters,
and things of the said corporation, as fully and effectually as if
thirteen of them had so convened, and shall have the like powers,
authorities, and interests, as by the said charter are given to and
vested in thirteen of the said Trustees or members, when duly convened; and shall be under the same directions, regulations, conditions, restrictions, provisos, and limitations, as to the benefit,
conveniency, and meetings of the said corporation, as are contained
in the said charter with respect to the quorum of thirteen Trustees
or members: PROVIDED ALWAYS, that the Governor of this State
for the time being, or in case of his death or absence, the President
of the said college for the time being, and in case of the death or
absence of both the said Governor and President, then the senior
Trustee of the said college shall always be one of the said nine
Trustees so at any time constituting a quorum as aforesaid.

*Nine to consti-
tute a quorum*

Proviso

6. AND BE IT ENACTED, That the said Trustees of the College
of New Jersey, and their successors, may have, hold, and enjoy

*Limitation of
value of estate*

---

* Repealed and supplied by Act of March 29th, 1866.

any estate whatsoever, the clear yearly value whereof shall not exceed *twenty thousand dollars.**

7. AND BE IT ENACTED, That the act entitled, "An act for amending and establishing the charter of the College of New Jersey," passed the thirteenth day of March, in the year of our Lord one thousand seven hundred and eighty, and the act entitled, "An act to continue an act entitled a supplemental act to an act entitled an act for amending and establishing the charter of the College of New Jersey," passed the twentieth day of November, in the year of our Lord one thousand seven hundred and eighty-six, be and they are hereby repealed.

Passed at Trenton, May 27th, 1799.

VI.

AN ACT further to amend the Charter of the College of New Jersey, being a supplement to an act entitled, "An act relative to the College of New Jersey." [March 11th, 1864.]

WHEREAS, It is represented on behalf of the Trustees of the College of New Jersey that they deem it important and desirable that the original intention and design of the founders of the college in establishing an institution for the promotion of religion, as well as the advancement of learning, should be distinctly recognized and established by law, and that it is necessary for the educational, charitable and other purposes of the institution, that the value of the property which the Trustees are authorized to hold should be increased ; therefore—

1. BE IT ENACTED BY THE SENATE AND GENERAL ASSEMBLY OF THE STATE OF NEW JERSEY, That the design and object of the said corporation is hereby declared to be the promotion of religion and the advancement of learning, by the instruction of youth in religious truth, as well as in the learned languages, and in the liberal arts and sciences, and that the said corporation shall always be an institution for the purposes specified in this act.

* See foot-note, p. 15.

2. AND BE IT ENACTED, That it shall be lawful for the Trustees of the College of New Jersey to take and receive by gift, grant, devise, or purchase, and to have, hold, and enjoy for the uses and purposes of the said corporation, including the tuition and support of indigent young men, any real and personal estate, the clear yearly income whereof shall not exceed *one hundred thousand dollars,* PROVIDED ALWAYS, that whenever any property or estate shall be given, granted, or devised to them upon any special trust, or for any special use or purpose not incompatible with the object and design of said corporation as above declared, that such property or estate shall be held and appropriated by them in strict accordance with the trust, uses, and limitations in such grants and devises respectively mentioned and set forth.

Passed at Trenton, March 11th, 1864.

May receive and hold gifts and grants

Limitation of value of estate

VII.

A FURTHER SUPPLEMENT to the Charter of the College of New Jersey.
March 29th, 1866.]

1. BE IT ENACTED BY THE SENATE AND GENERAL ASSEMBLY OF THE STATE OF NEW JERSEY, That if any person shall be elected a Trustee or officer of said corporation he shall, before he enters upon the duties of his office, take and subscribe an oath or affirmation faithfully and impartially to perform the duties of his office ; an oath to support the Constitution of the United States ; and the oath of allegiance to the State in which he resides ; and that the said oaths may be administered by any member of said corporation.

Oaths to be taken by trustees and officers

2. AND BE IT ENACTED, That it shall be lawful for said college to confer any degrees granted by any other college or university.

Degrees

3. AND BE IT ENACTED, That the fourth section of the supplement passed May twenty-ninth, seventeen hundred and ninety-nine, be, and the same is hereby, repealed.

Repealing clause

Passed at Trenton, March 29th, 1866.

---

*Altered to *five hundred thousand dollars*, June 26th, 1889. See foot-note, p. 15.

VIII.

AN ACT further to amend the Charter of the College of New Jersey
[April 6th, 1868.]

1. BE IT ENACTED BY THE SENATE AND GENERAL ASSEMBLY OF THE STATE OF NEW JERSEY, That the number of Trustees of the College of New Jersey may be increased to twenty-seven whenever the Board of Trustees shall by a vote of two-thirds determine upon such increase.

2. AND BE IT ENACTED, That this act shall take effect immediately.

Passed at Trenton, April 6th, 1868.

IX.

GENERAL ACT.

AN ACT to authorize corporations organized for religious, educational or benevolent purposes to procure an increase of their capacity to acquire and hold real and personal property. [March 27th, 1889.]

1. BE IT ENACTED BY THE SENATE AND GENERAL ASSEMBLY OF THE STATE OF NEW JERSEY, That whenever any corporation of this State, incorporated for religious, educational or benevolent purposes, shall, by its charter or any supplement thereto, or otherwise, be limited in the amount or value of real or personal property which it may acquire, have, hold and enjoy for the use and purposes of such corporation, and the board of trustees, directors or managers of such corporation shall desire to obtain for such corporation legal capacity to acquire, have, hold, use and enjoy a larger amount than that to which it is or shall be so limited, that it shall be lawful for such trustees, directors or managers at any stated meeting of said board, and from time to time, to adopt by vote of a majority of the whole number of such trustees, directors or managers, a resolution declaring their desire to have the amount so enlarged, and stating the amount to which it is to be so increased, and to cause a copy of such resolution, authenticated and verified as by this act directed, to be filed in the office of the secretary of state.

2. AND BE IT ENACTED, That the copy of the resolution authorized by the first section of this act to be filed with the secretary of state, shall be certified and authenticated under the common seal of said corporation, and shall be verified by the oath of the clerk or secretary of said corporation that the seal affixed to said copy is the common seal of said corporation, that the said copy is a true copy of the original resolution as recorded on the minutes of said board, and that it was passed as directed in the first section of this act.

3. AND BE IT ENACTED, That on filing said copy of such resolution in the office of the secretary of state, it shall be thereafter lawful for the said corporation to take and receive by gift, grant, devise, bequest or purchase, and to have, hold and enjoy for the uses and purposes of the said corporation any real or personal estate not exceeding the increased amount named in said resolution, any provision of the charter of said corporation, or any supplement thereto, to the contrary notwithstanding.

4. AND BE IT ENACTED, That this act shall be a public act and shall take effect immediately.

Approved March 27th, 1889.

PREAMBLE AND RESOLUTION ADOPTED BY A MAJORITY OF THE WHOLE NUMBER OF THE TRUSTEES OF THE COLLEGE OF NEW JERSEY, JUNE 17TH, 1889.

WHEREAS, THE TRUSTEES OF THE COLLEGE OF NEW JERSEY, a corporation of the State of New Jersey, incorporated for educational purposes, by a supplement to their charter, are limited in the value of the real and personal property they may lawfully acquire, have, hold and enjoy for the uses and purposes of said incorporation, to an amount the clear yearly income whereof shall not exceed one hundred thousand dollars; which said sum is totally inadequate to meet the urgent and imperative needs of the .corporation : Therefore be it—

RESOLVED, That it is, and by this resolution it is declared to be, the desire of the said Trustees to obtain the legal capacity to take, acquire, have, hold and enjoy a larger amount of real and personal property than that to which they are so limited as aforesaid ; to wit, an amount that shall yield a clear yearly income of five hundred thousand dollars.

I, Elijah R. Craven, Clerk of the Trustees of the College of New Jersey, do hereby certify that the foregoing preamble and resolution were, at a stated meeting of the Board of Trustees of the College of New Jersey, held at Princeton, New Jersey, on the seventeenth day of June, A. D. eighteen hundred and eighty-nine, adopted by vote of a majority of the whole number of said Trustees.

(Signed),   E. R. CRAVEN,

Clerk of The Trustees of The College of New Jersey.

AFFIDAVIT OF THE CLERK OF "THE TRUSTEES OF THE COLLEGE OF NEW JERSEY."

[June 26, 1889.]

STATE OF NEW JERSEY, *ss.*

Be it known that on this twenty-sixth day of June, A. D. eighteen hundred and eighty-nine, before me, one of the masters of the Court of Chancery of the State of New Jersey, personally appeared Elijah R. Craven, who being by me duly sworn upon his oath saith—that he is the Clerk of "The Trustees of the College of New Jersey"; that the seal affixed to the foregoing resolution is the common seal of said corporation; that said resolution is a true copy of the original resolution as recorded in the minutes of said Board of Trustees; and that said original resolution was passed as directed in the first section of an act entitled, "An Act to authorize corporations organized for religious, educational or benevolent purposes to procure an increase of their capacity to acquire and hold real and personal property," approved March 27th, 1889.

(Signed),   LEWIS PARKER,
                                     Master in Chancery of N. J.

ENDORSED.   "Filed June 26, 1889,
             HENRY C. KELSEY,
                 Secretary of State."

CERTIFICATE OF THE SECRETARY OF STATE.

STATE OF NEW JERSEY,⎱
DEPARTMENT OF STATE.⎰

I, HENRY C. KELSEY, Secretary of State of the State of New Jersey, do hereby certify, that the foregoing is a true copy of RESOLUTION adopted by "THE TRUSTEES OF THE COLLEGE OF NEW JERSEY" to procure an increase of capacity to acquire and hold real and personal property, as the same is taken from and compared with the original (filed June 26, 1889), and now remaining on file in my office.

IN TESTIMONY WHEREOF, I have hereunto set my hand and affixed my Official Seal, at Trenton, this First day of July, A. D. 1890.

(Signed).   HENRY C. KELSEY,
                    Secretary of State.

X.

GENERAL ACT.

A SUPPLEMENT to an act entitled "An Act to Incorporate Societies for the Promotion of Learning" (Revision), approved April ninth, one thousand eight hundred and seventy-five. [March 16th, 1893.]

1. BE IT ENACTED BY THE SENATE AND GENERAL ASSEMBLY OF THE STATE OF NEW JERSEY, That the trustees of any seminary, college, school or other institution now or hereafter organized under the act to which this is the supplement, or any other act now in force in this State, may purchase, take, hold, receive and enjoy all lands, tenements and hereditaments, in fee simple or otherwise, and also all goods, chattels, legacies and donations, in money or otherwise, of what kind or nature soever, that may be granted and conveyed or given and devised to the seminary or other institution of which they shall be trustees, as aforesaid, by the grant, gift, alienation or devise of any person or persons able to grant, give or devise the same for the support, endowment or otherwise, of said seminary or school, whether in general or for particular chairs or departments thereof, or for special objects or subjects taught therein ; and also that the said trustees and their successors shall and may grant, assign and sell, or otherwise dispose of all or any of their said lands, tenements or hereditaments, goods, chattels and personal estate whatsoever, received and

Trustees authorized to purchase property, also receive goods granted, devised, etc.

Trustees authorized to dispose of property, unless otherwise provided

held by them as aforesaid, as to them shall seem meet for the best interests of their said seminary or other institution, unless otherwise provided and limited by the deeds, wills, or other instruments in writing by which they received and hold the same ; *provided, nevertheless*, that the proceeds of the sale or other disposition of any real or personal estate so received and held by such trustees for said endowment objects or purposes shall be duly re-invested in other good real or personal estate, as soon thereafter as practicable, and the annual income therefrom only used for such endowment and educational purposes.

2. AND BE IT ENACTED, That this act shall take effect immediately.

Approved March 16, 1893.

XI.

GENERAL ACT.

A SUPPLEMENT TO AN ACT entitled, " An Act to Incorporate Societies for the Promotion of Learning " [Revision], approved April ninth, one thousand eight hundred and seventy-five. [April 12, 1894.]

Incorporated institutions of learning may change corporate name

1. BE IT ENACTED BY THE SENATE AND GENERAL ASSEMBLY OF THE STATE OF NEW JERSEY, That it shall be lawful for any association, seminary, college or other institution of learning now or hereafter organized under and by virtue of the act to which this is a supplement, or any other act now in force in this State, whether created by special charter or otherwise, to change its corporate name by a two-thirds vote of the board of trustees or managers of such association, seminary, college or other institution of learning who shall be present at a regular or special meeting of the same,

Proviso

called for that purpose ; *provided*, that said corporation cause to be made and filed a certificate in writing, in manner hereinafter

Certificate shall set forth new name and be filed and recorded in county clerk's office

mentioned ; such certificate shall set forth, first, the name of said association, seminary, college or other institution of learning in use immediately preceding said vote and making and filing of said certificate ; second, the new name assumed to designate such corporation and to be used in its business and dealings in the place and stead of that referred to in the last preceding paragraph, and which said certificate shall be signed by said board of trustees or managers, or a majority thereof, and filed and recorded in the office of the clerk of the county where the principal office or place of business of such corporation in this State shall be established; and after being so recorded shall be filed in the office of the secretary of state, without fee or costs; and to which said certificate shall be affixed the official seal of said board of trustees or managers, and the affidavit of the secretary or acting secretary of said board that he said certificate is made by the authority of the board of trustees or managers of such corporation, as expressed by a two-thirds vote of the members present at a regular or special meeting of said board called for that purpose.

And also secretary of state's office

Shall be verified by official seal and affidavit

2. AND BE IT ENACTED, That no change in the name of any corporation, under the provisions of this act, shall be deemed effected until the said certificate, made and recorded as aforesaid, shall be actually filed in the office of the secretary of state, as herein directed; but no such change shall in any manner lessen or impair any liability of such corporation incurred or existing at the time such change of name shall be made, which liability shall continue and be capable of being enforced against such corporation by its name as so changed, or by its original name; and no suit pending at the time of such change of name shall abate by reason thereof, but the same may be prosecuted to judgment and execution in the original name of such corporation, and under such execution the property of said corporation, whether held by its original or amended name, may be levied on and sold to satisfy such judgment.

No change of name shall be effectual until conditions are complied with

Existing liabilities not to be impaired

3. AND BE IT ENACTED, That all acts and part of acts inconsistent with this act be and the same are hereby repealed, and that his act shall take effect immediately.

Repealer

Approved April 12, 1894.

XII.

CERTIFICATE OF CHANGE OF CORPORATE NAME.

(February 13th, 1896.)

The Trustees of the College of New Jersey, a college corporation, being an institution of learning organized under and by virtue of Letters Patent of his Majesty George the Second, King of Great Britain, France and Ireland, granted and issued by Jonathan Belcher, Esquire, Governor and Commander in Chief of the Province of New Jersey, September fourteenth, 1748, and established by acts of the Legislature of New Jersey, now in force in this State, doth hereby certify that at a regular meeting of the Board of Trustees of said corporation, called (among other things) for the purpose of changing the corporate name of said College or Institution of learning, the said Board of Trustees, by a two-thirds vote of the members present at said meeting, resolved to change the name of said corporation to "The Trustees of Princeton University"; and to that end the said corporation doth certify and set forth :

(1.) That the name of said corporation in use immediately preceding the said vote, and the making and filing of this certificate, was "The Trustees of the College of New Jersey."

(2.) The new name assumed to designate said corporation, and to be used in its business and dealings in the place and stead of that mentioned in the last preceding paragraph, is "The Trustees of Princeton University."

In WITNESS WHEREOF, the said The Trustees of the College of New Jersey, hath caused the official seal of said Board of Trustees, being also the common seal of said corporation, to be hereunto affixed ; and the undersigned, being a majority of said Board of Trustees, have hereunto set their signatures, all this thirteenth day of February, in the year of our Lord one thousand eight hundred and ninety-six.

FRANCIS L. PATTON, *President.*

E. R. CRAVEN,	JAMES W. ALEXANDER,
HENRY M. ALEXANDER,	F. B. HODGE,
WILLIAM M. PAXTON,	D. R. FRAZER,
JOHN A. STEWART,	JOHN K. COWEN,
JOHN HALL,	GEORGE B. STEWART,
W. HENRY GREEN,	CYRUS H. McCORMICK,
CHARLES E. GREEN,	M. W. JACOBUS,
THOMAS N. McCARTER,	W. J. MAGIE,
S. BAYARD DOD,	EDW. T. GREEN,
J. ADDISON HENRY,	JOHN J. McCOOK,
M. TAYLOR PYNE,	JOHN DIXON.

STATE OF NEW JERSEY, }
COUNTY OF MERCER, } ss.:

Elijah R. Craven, Secretary (otherwise known and designated as Clerk) of the Trustees of the College of New Jersey, being duly sworn on his oath, says: That the foregoing certificate is made by authority of the Board of Trustees of said corporation, as expressed by a two-thirds vote of the members present at a regular meeting of said Board, called (among other things) for that purpose.

Sworn to and subscribed before me, this } E. R. CRAVEN.
thirteenth day of February, A. D. 1896. }

E. C. OSBORN,
Notary Public.

Received in the office of the Clerk of the County of Mercer, State of New Jersey, on the 27th day of May, A. D. 1896, and recorded in Book C. of Corporations for said County, page 369.

Filed in the office of the Secretary of State, October 22d, 1896.

H. C. KELSEY,
Secretary.

By-Laws.

Adopted March 9th, 1899.

Index of By-Laws.

By-Laws

OF THE BOARD OF TRUSTEES.

CHAPTER I.

OF THE TRUSTEES GENERALLY.

1. THE BOARD SHALL CONSIST OF NOT MORE THAN TWENTY-SEVEN PERSONS, INCLUDING THE GOVERNOR OF THE STATE AND THE PRESIDENT OF THE UNIVERSITY DURING THEIR RESPECTIVE OFFICIAL TERMS.

2. OF THE ENTIRE BOARD, TWELVE SHALL BE INHABITANTS OF THE STATE OF NEW JERSEY.

3. THE TRUSTEES, WITH THE EXCEPTION OF THE GOVERNOR OF THE STATE, SHALL HOLD OFFICE DURING THEIR NATURAL LIVES, SAVE IN CASE OF RESIGNATION OR REMOVAL WITH CAUSE BY THE BOARD.

4. EACH TRUSTEE, BEFORE HE ENTERS UPON THE DUTIES OF HIS OFFICE, SHALL TAKE AND SUBSCRIBE AN OATH OR AFFIRMATION, FAITHFULLY AND IMPARTIALLY TO PERFORM THE DUTIES OF HIS OFFICE, AN OATH TO SUPPORT THE CONSTITUTION OF THE UNITED STATES, AND AN OATH OF ALLEGIANCE TO THE STATE IN WHICH HE RESIDES. THE SAID OATHS SHALL BE TAKEN IN THE PRESENCE OF THE BOARD, AND MAY BE ADMINISTERED BY ANY MEMBER OF SAID CORPORATION.

5. Of the ordinary members of the Board, twelve at least shall be clergymen, and twelve at least shall be laymen, save when, for reasons of expediency, it may be proper to alter this proportion, in which case, the proportionate numbers shall be restored as soon as practicable.

6. Whenever a vacancy in the Board occurs, a new Trustee shall be elected by ballot, by the affirmative votes of not less than a majority of the entire Board of Trustees. Such election, however, shall not take place at the session of the Board at which the nomination of the candidate to fill such vacancy is made, although it may take place at the same meeting.

7. If any Trustee be absent from four consecutive stated meetings of the Board, for which absence he shall present no excuse satisfactory to the Board, his seat shall be regarded as vacated, save by a special vote of the Board to the contrary.

CHAPTER II.

OF MEETINGS OF THE BOARD.

8. There shall be four Stated Meetings of the Board of Trustees each year; the first or Commencement Meeting, on the Monday preceding the Commencement; the second on the day preceding Commemoration day; the third on the second Thursday in December; and the fourth on the second Thursday in March.

9. SPECIAL MEETINGS SHALL BE HELD UPON THE REQUISITION OF SIX TRUSTEES, MADE UPON THE CLERK. This requisition shall specify the object for which the meeting is called, and such object shall be stated by the Clerk in his notice of the meeting; and no business shall be transacted at such special meeting other than that specified in the requisition and mentioned in the notice.

10. ANY NINE OR MORE OF THE TRUSTEES, WHEN DULY CONVENED, SHALL CONSTITUTE A QUORUM, AND BE COMPETENT TO PERFORM AND EXECUTE ALL THE DUTIES, BUSINESS MATTERS AND THINGS OF THE SAID CORPORATION, PROVIDED ALWAYS, THAT THE GOVERNOR OF THE STATE FOR THE TIME BEING, OR IN CASE OF HIS DEATH OR ABSENCE, THE PRESIDENT OF THE UNIVERSITY FOR THE TIME BEING; AND IN CASE OF THE DEATH OR ABSENCE OF BOTH THE GOVERNOR AND PRESIDENT, THE SENIOR TRUSTEE OF THE SAID UNIVERSITY SHALL ALWAYS BE ONE OF THE SAID NINE TRUSTEES, SO AT ANY TIME CONSTITUTING THE QUORUM AS AFORESAID; BUT IN CASE OF THE ABSENCE OF THE GOVERNOR OF

THE STATE, THE PRESIDENT OF THE UNIVERSITY AND THE SENIOR TRUSTEE, THEN THIRTEEN MEMBERS SHALL CONSTITUTE A QUORUM.

11. NO MEETING OF THE TRUSTEES SHALL BE VALID OR LEGAL FOR THE TRANSACTION OF ANY BUSINESS WHATEVER, UNLESS THE CLERK OF THE BOARD HAS DULY AND LEGALLY NOTIFIED EACH AND EVERY MEMBER OF THE CORPORATION OF SUCH MEETING; AND BEFORE THEIR ENTERING UPON ANY BUSINESS, THE CLERK SHALL CERTIFY SUCH NOTIFICATION, UNDER HIS HAND, TO THE BOARD OF TRUSTEES.

12. The Clerk shall give notice of each meeting of the Board at least one week before the appointed time thereof.

13. Any number convened, at the time of a meeting, less than a quorum, and more than two, may adjourn from time to time, for a period of three days; after which time they may adjourn to a period not less than one week distant, of which adjourned meeting due notice shall be given by the Clerk.

14. Each meeting of the Board shall be opened with prayer.

15. Trustees shall sit, when in session, in the order of seniority, beginning at the right hand of the President.

CHAPTER III.

OF THE OFFICERS OF THE BOARD.

16. The officers of the Board shall be the Presiding Officer, President of the University, Clerk, Dean of the Faculty, Treasurer, Secretary, Curator of Grounds and Buildings, Librarian, Registrar, and such other officers as the Board may deem it expedient to appoint.

17. THESE OFFICERS, with the exception of the Presiding Officer, SHALL BE ELECTED BY THE BOARD, AND SHALL CONTINUE IN OFFICE DURING THE PLEASURE OF THE BOARD, AND THEY SHALL RECEIVE SUCH COMPENSATION AS THE BOARD MAY DIRECT.

CHAPTER IV.

OF THE PRESIDING OFFICER.

18. THE GOVERNOR OF THE STATE OF NEW JERSEY SHALL BE, ex officio, PRESIDENT OF THE BOARD, AND IN HIS ABSENCE

THE PRESIDENT OF THE UNIVERSITY SHALL PRESIDE, AND IN THE ABSENCE OF THE GOVERNOR AND PRESIDENT OF THE UNIVERSITY, THE SENIOR TRUSTEE, PRESENT AT ANY MEETING, SHALL PRESIDE.

19. It shall be the duty of the Presiding Officer to observe the order of business, and enforce the rules of order.

CHAPTER V.

OF THE PRESIDENT OF THE UNIVERSITY (IN HIS RELATION TO THE BOARD).

20. The President of the University shall be elected by ballot, by a majority of the entire Board of Trustees. The election of any person to the office of President, shall not take place until at least the day following his nomination.

21. IN THE ABSENCE OF THE GOVERNOR OF THE STATE, HE SHALL PRESIDE AT THE MEETINGS OF THE BOARD.

22. He shall preside on all public occasions, and represent the University before the public.

23. He shall be charged with the general supervision of the interests of the University and shall have special oversight of the various departments of instruction in the University.

24. It shall be his duty to sign all obligations and contracts entered into by or on behalf of the Board, unless otherwise provided by these By-Laws.

25. He shall have the custody of the Seal of the University and affix the same to such instruments as require its use.

26. He shall present a printed report at each stated meeting of the Board, of the condition of the University in respect of such matters as he may deem necessary. The different subjects embraced in his report shall be referred to the appropriate Standing Committees having charge of the same. He shall make annually to the Board a report of the condition, progress and policy of the University, which shall include reports to him by such of the University officers as may, in the judgment of the Board, be deemed best.

CHAPTER VI.

OF THE CLERK.

27. The Clerk shall always be a member of the Board of Trustees.

28. IT SHALL BE HIS DUTY TO NOTIFY THE TRUSTEES OF ALL MEETINGS, AND TO CERTIFY THE FACT OF SUCH NOTICE HAVING BEEN GIVEN AT THE OPENING OF EACH MEETING OF THE BOARD.

29. He shall be the custodian of the Charter of the Institution, of the minute books and papers relating to the records of the University, and of the Bond of the Treasurer.

30. He shall keep full minutes of the meetings of the Board, and at each stated meeting shall present the minutes of the last preceding meeting or meetings, fairly written, for the approval of the Board. When such minutes are approved by the Board, they shall be engrossed in the book of minutes.

31. He shall notify, by letter, all persons elected to office by the Board, and those receiving Honorary Degrees of the fact that such degrees have been conferred upon them.

32. As soon as possible after each meeting, he shall transmit to the President of the University, the Dean, the Treasurer, the Clerk of the Faculty, and the Chairman of each Standing and Special Committee, all papers, matters, resolutions, or business, that have been referred respectively to the President, the Dean, the Treasurer, the Faculty, or such Committee.

33. He shall, when he gives notice to the Chairman of a Special Committee of the duties required by resolution of the Board, request such Chairman to inform him of the meeting of the Committee. If within two weeks of the meeting of the Board he shall not have been informed of the meeting of a Committee whose Chairman has been notified, he shall again notify such Chairman.

34. At least one week before each stated meeting he shall transmit to each member of the Board a printed copy of the docket of the business that will come before said meeting.

35. He may, with the approbation of the Board, appoint an assistant to aid him in his duties, and to supply his place when absent, which assistant shall receive such compensation as the Board may direct.

36. In case of the death, absence, or disability of the Clerk, the President of the University, or the Dean in case of the death, absence, or disability of the President, shall be, *ex officio*, Clerk of the Board, for the purpose of notifying the Trustees of meetings.

CHAPTER VII.

OF THE DEAN OF THE FACULTY.

37. The Dean of the Faculty shall be elected by ballot, by a majority of the entire Board of Trustees. The election shall not take place at the sitting of the Board at which the nomination is presented, although the nomination and election may be made at the same meeting.

38. He shall be charged with the oversight of whatever does not pertain directly to the work of instruction, such in particular as the discipline of the University, the assignment of rooms in the dormitories to Instructors and Fellows, and the sanitary condition of the Institution :—and to this end he shall be a member, *ex officio*, of the Committee on Morals and Discipline ; the Curator of Grounds and Buildings shall report to him upon questions of discipline so far as they may come under his notice and as to the health of the students ; and the Proctors shall be subordinated to him as well as to the President of the University, and shall report to him on all matters relating to the deportment of the students.

39. He shall report in writing to the Committee on Morals and Discipline at each stated meeting of the Board of Trustees on the state of discipline in the University, and on all matters relating thereto.

CHAPTER VIII.

OF THE TREASURER.

40. The Treasurer shall have charge and supervision, under direction of the Committee on Finance, of all the securities and funds of the Corporation.

41. He shall sign receipts and acknowledgments for all money and other property of the Corporation, and disburse the money under the direction of the Finance Committee.

42. He shall deposit the funds of the University in the corporate name of the University, in such banks or trust companies as the Finance Committee shall direct; which funds shall not be drawn out except by checks signed by him, and, when for sums exceeding two thousand dollars, countersigned by a member of the Finance Committee, or by some person specially designated by the Finance Committee for that purpose.

43. He shall render a full and particular statement of his cash accounts, accompanied by vouchers, and an inventory of the investments of the Corporation, to the Finance Committee, at least one week prior to each December and March meeting of the Board.

44. His books shall be open at all reasonable times to the inspection of members of the Finance Committee.

45. He may be authorized by the Board to employ necessary assistants when the funds of the University permit.

46. He shall give bonds for the faithful performance of his duties, in such amount as the Board shall direct.

CHAPTER IX.

OF THE CURATOR OF GROUNDS AND BUILDINGS.

47. The Curator of Grounds and Buildings shall be the Resident Executive of the Committee on Grounds and Buildings of the Board of Trustees.

48. He shall, under the supervision of the Committee on Grounds and Buildings, have charge and control of the real estate

belonging to the University; and he shall be responsible for the proper care and maintenance of the same.

49. He shall, subject as aforesaid, and subject also to such other Committee or Committees having supervision of the same, have charge and control of, and be responsible for, the proper care and maintenance of all the personal property belonging to the University, except the securities and funds, and the apparatus and specimens belonging to the several departments of instruction, and the books in the Library. And as to these last named, excepting the securities and funds, he shall take such charge and perform such duties as the Committees having supervision of the same shall require.

50. He shall, subject to said supervision, have sole charge of all repairs to the Grounds and Buildings belonging to the University, and shall be responsible for the keeping of the same in repair and in order. All requests for repairs, or work of any kind, shall be made to him in writing, and be signed by the person making the request upon blanks which the Curator shall furnish for the purpose; and the Curator shall enter such requests, or copy the same, in a book to be kept for the purpose, with the date of the request, and what disposition he has made of the request and the date of the same—which book shall at all times be open to the inspection of the members of the Faculty and of the Committee on Grounds and Buildings.

51. He shall make no alteration in any building, or in any part of the grounds, and shall take no action in reference to the personal property confided to his care, unless he shall first obtain the consent of the Committee having charge of the same.

52. No alteration shall be made in any building belonging to the University, by any one, except under the direction of the Curator, and not by him unless the consent of the proper Committee shall first be obtained.

53. He shall, subject to the aforesaid supervision, have the sole charge of the sewerage and drainage of the University Grounds and Buildings.

54. He shall, subject to the aforesaid supervision, have the sole charge and responsibility of the lighting and heating apparatus of the University, and shall make all contracts for gas and the purchase of coal and other fuel.

55. He shall, subject to the aforesaid supervision, have the sole charge and management of the water supply of the University.

56. He shall audit all bills for labor and materials furnished the University in his department.

57. He shall, subject to the supervision aforesaid, make all contracts for work to be done on the grounds and buildings, except for new buildings otherwise provided for.

58. The employment, oversight and direction of all University servants shall be committed to him.

59. He shall keep under constant inspection the grounds and buildings belonging to the University, and be responsible that the former are kept in good order, and that the rooms, entries, cellars, roofs, and every other part of said buildings, are kept clean and in good repair, and that snow is early removed whenever the same is necessary.

60. Upon receiving from the Sanitary Committee of the Faculty any written opinion or suggestion referring to the health of the University, he shall forthwith communicate the same to the proper Committee having the subject in charge.

61. Whenever in the opinion of the Curator any student should be removed from a room or University dormitory, for what, to the Curator, seems a proper cause, he shall report the same to the Dean for the action of the Faculty.

62. He shall charge students and employees of the University for damage to University property, and should any student refuse to pay the damage assessed by the Curator, he shall at once report the fact to the Dean for the action of the Faculty.

63. Whenever any dereliction of duty on the part of any employee of the University shall be reported to him by the President, Dean, a professor, student, or other person, he shall promptly examine the matter and adopt such steps as the case warrants.

64. He shall, at the beginning of every fiscal year, make an estimate in writing of every expense which will probably arise in his department during the ensuing year; striving to make the expenses of his department as small as possible, consistent with the proper care and maintenance of the property.

65. He shall decide in what houses, outside of the University dormitories, students may room and board. In no case shall he permit a student to reside or board in a house, if the Sanitary Committee of the Faculty shall notify him in writing that they object to such house.

66. The Curator shall adopt such a system as will enable him to know at once if there is a case of illness in any University dormitory, or in any house in which students reside, and shall immediately report to the Dean, or, in the absence of the Dean, to the Chairman or Secretary of the Sanitary Committee of the Faculty.

67. He shall, within a reasonable time after receiving any written opinion or suggestion from the Sanitary Committee of the Faculty, inform the Chairman of said Committee, in writing, what action has been taken in reference to such opinion or suggestion.

68. He shall perform such other duties as shall be assigned to him by the Board and the several Committees.

CHAPTER X.

OF THE LIBRARY AND THE LIBRARIAN.

69. The Librarian and any members of the Library staff holding rank equivalent to that of Members of the Faculty shall be chosen in the same manner as officers of instruction and government. The Librarian shall have the care of the Library, under the direction of the Committee on the Library and Apparatus. He shall be responsible for the safe keeping, proper treatment and prompt exhibition of everything hereby committed to his care.

70. He shall annually report to the Trustees the condition of the Library, including his expenditure for books, binding and periodicals; the accessions by purchase and by donation; the

loans of books, and such other facts as may seem deserving their attention. He shall also permanently record these reports.

71. Two-thirds of the annual revenue on the Elizabeth foundation for the purchase of books shall be expended by the Librarian, under the direction of the Faculty. The remaining third of this revenue shall be expended at the discretion of the Librarian, subject to the approval of the Committee on the Library and Apparatus.

CHAPTER XI.

OF THE REGISTRAR.

72. It shall be the duty of the Registrar to keep the record of the examinations and standing of the students, and to report the same twice in each year to their parents or guardians.

73. He shall keep the record of the attendance of each student upon the University exercises and take such action thereon as the regulations pertaining to students require.

74. He shall conduct such correspondence with the parents and guardians, concerning the attendance and scholarship of students, as the Faculty or its Committees may instruct, or as the circumstances of each case may require.

75. He shall conduct the correspondence relating to the admission of students to the University, and have charge of the distribution of the University catalogue.

CHAPTER XII.

OF THE FACULTY.

76. The University Faculty shall consist of the President, Dean, Professors and Assistant Professors. The University Faculty shall be divided into two sub-Faculties, to be designated respectively as the Academic Faculty and the Scientific Faculty. The Academic Faculty shall consist of the Professors and Assistant Professors whose duties pertain wholly, or in the main, to the Academic Department, and the Scientific Faculty shall consist of the Professors and Assistant Professors whose duties pertain wholly, or

in the main, to the John C. Green School of Science. The proceedings of the sub-Faculties shall be regularly reported to the University Faculty, and in all ordinary cases the action of each sub-Faculty, in respect to the admission, standing and discipline of students, shall be final.

77. Professors and Assistant Professors shall be elected by ballot—and no election shall take place at the sitting of the Board at which the person so to be elected is nominated, although the nomination and election may be at the same meeting.

78. Tutors, Instructors, Lecturers and Readers shall be appointed by the Board, and shall have the privilege of sitting with the Faculty, but shall not be entitled to vote.

79. Officers of instruction shall not substitute or appoint any one to perform their duties in the class-room without the approval, in each case, of the President.

80. The University Faculty shall keep a book of minutes, which book shall be laid before the Board of Trustees at each of its stated meetings, and shall be referred to the Committees on the Curriculum, and on Morals and Discipline.

81. The University Faculty shall, before each stated meeting of the Board, elect, by ballot, three Professors, two from the Academic and one from the Scientific Faculty, who shall attend and present to the Board the views of the Faculty on matters pertaining to the instruction, order, and government of the University.

CHAPTER XIII.

OF THE STANDING COMMITTEES OF THE BOARD.

82. The Board, at its stated June meeting, shall appoint, by ballot, the following six Standing Committees, each consisting of not more than nine members, including the President or Dean of the Faculty, who shall hold their office for one year and until others are appointed in their place :

1. A Committee on Finance.
2. A Committee on Grounds and Buildings.
3. A Committee on the Library and Apparatus.

4. A Committee on the Curriculum.
5. A Committee on Morals and Discipline.
6. A Committee on Honorary Degrees.

83. The President of the University shall be, *ex officio*, a member of the first five named of these Committees and the Chairman of the Committee on Honorary Degrees ; and the Dean of the Faculty shall be, *ex officio*, a member of the Committee on Morals and Discipline.

84. At the March meeting of the Board in each year the Presiding Officer shall appoint a committee of five members of the Board, to whom may be presented suggestions for changes in the composition of the several Standing Committees. This Committee shall report at the June meeting its recommendations as to how the Standing Committees shall be constituted for the year following.

85. Each Committee shall be empowered to elect its own Chairman, and no Trustee, other than the President of the University, shall be a member of more than three of these Committees, and no Trustee shall be Chairman of more than one Standing Committee. If a Trustee be elected as Chairman of more than one Standing Committee, he shall have the privilege of selection.

86. Each Standing Committee shall meet at least four times a year, and at such other times as may be ordered by the Board, or may be called together by the Chairman ; and the Chairman shall always call a meeting of the Committee on the requisition of the President of the University, or of three members of the Board. One week's notice of each meeting shall be given, except that in cases of emergency, meetings of the Committee on Finance or Grounds and Buildings may be called upon shorter notice.

87. Any number, not less than three, shall constitute a quorum for the transaction of business.

88. Each Standing Committee shall report in writing at each stated meeting of the Board, and the reports shall be recorded by the Clerk of the Board in books provided for the purpose.

89. The Chairman of each Committee shall be in readiness to report at the opening of the meeting of the Board.

CHAPTER XIV.

OF THE COMMITTEE ON FINANCE.

90. It shall be the duty of the Committee on Finance to supervise the funds and securities of the Corporation.

91. They shall keep a careful oversight of the investments of the Corporation, and shall report to the Board their judgment as to the investment of the funds, and the changes that should be made.

92. Should any funds accrue during an *interim* of the Board they shall have power to invest the same, making a report of such investment at the next stated meeting.

93. If at any time during an *interim* of the Board they should deem it essential to the interests of the University that a change of investments be made, they shall have the power to make such change and to direct the transfer, if the investments to be changed are in registered securities, and they shall always report the fact of such change and the reason thereof to the Board at its next stated meeting.

94. They shall inform themselves whenever any interest upon the securities of the University has failed to be paid, and proceed to collect the same.

95. They shall see that no contracts are made for the payment of money, unless the money is arranged for beforehand; and no distinct fund shall be borrowed from, for any other use than that for which it is designated, unless by a vote of the Board.

96. They shall, at least once a year, examine the securities of the Corporation, and report the result of such examination to the Board.

97. They shall designate in writing to the Treasurer in what banks or trust companies the cash of the Corporation shall be deposited, and in what depository the securities of the same shall be kept.

98. They shall designate a person to sign the checks of the Corporation with the Treasurer, as provided for in Chapter VIII., Article 45.

99. Expenditures authorized by any of the Standing Committees shall not be made, if it be certified by the Committee on

Finance to the Treasurer that there are no moneys available for the purpose.

100. They shall appoint an Auditing Committee of two or more members of the Board, who shall carefully audit the accounts of the Treasurer, verify his statements, and report upon the same to the Committee twice in each year, which report, together with the Treasurer's Report, the Committee shall present to the Board at the stated meetings in October and March.

CHAPTER XV.

OF THE COMMITTEE ON GROUNDS AND BUILDINGS.

101. The Committee on University Grounds and Buildings shall have the supervision of the real estate, buildings and furniture belonging to the University, excepting as mentioned in Chapter XVI., Article 110.

102. They shall, at least once in each year, examine each building.

103. They shall instruct the Curator of Grounds and Buildings as to what repairs are necessary, and shall give him such power as they think necessary to enable him to attend to the care and repairs of the buildings, fences, real estate and furniture.

104. They shall have the supervision and control of the servants of the University, and shall instruct the Curator of Grounds and Buildings as to their number and compensation.

105. They shall be responsible that the Curator of Grounds and Buildings takes care of all matters in their department, and keeps the fences, drains, walks, offices and furniture, in proper condition.

106. They may authorize the Curator of Grounds and Buildings to act in cases where delay would work an injury.

CHAPTER XVI.

OF THE COMMITTEE ON THE LIBRARY AND APPARATUS.

107. The Committee on the Library and Apparatus shall have the supervision of the Library, Library buildings and all the apparatus used in the departments of instruction.

108. They shall have the direction of the Library, shall prescribe the times of opening and closing the same, and shall authorize the purchase of books in consistence with the By-Laws relating to the Librarian.

109. It shall be their duty to see that none of the property under their charge is lost or needlessly injured; and they shall hold the Librarian, Professors and Teachers, having charge of the same, to strict accountability in the premises.

110. The expenses of all new and movable property, chemicals and apparatus, and all repairs of the same, shall be authorized by the Committee, to the extent only of the appropriations made by the Board.

CHAPTER XVII.

OF THE COMMITTEE ON THE CURRICULUM.

111. The Committee on the Curriculum shall have charge of the studies pursued in the University.

112. They shall assign the duties of the Professors, and the time which shall be allotted to each branch of the studies.

113. They shall report to the Board what changes may be desirable in both the Academic Department and the School of Science.

114. They shall receive from the Faculty the names of candidates for Degrees in Course, and examine and report to the Board the names of those whom they recommend for such Degrees.

CHAPTER XVIII.

OF THE COMMITTEE ON MORALS AND DISCIPLINE.

115. The Committee on Morals and Discipline shall acquaint themselves thoroughly with the plans for discipline pursued in this and other Universities, and shall suggest to the Trustees and Faculty such plans as may, in their opinion, be of advantage to the University. Before each stated meeting of the Board they shall confer with the Dean regarding the discipline of the University

and make a report to the Board thereon, which deals practically with the then present disciplinary condition of the University.

116. They may be consulted by the Faculty on the best means of managing the discipline of the University and the preservation of the morals of the Institution.

CHAPTER XIX.

OF THE COMMITTEE ON HONORARY DEGREES.

117. To the Committee on Honorary Degrees all nominations for Honorary Degrees made in the Board shall be sent to be investigated and reported on to the Board, unless otherwise ordered by the unanimous vote of the members present, in number not less than a majority of the entire Board.

118. They shall, on recommending a person for a particular Degree, set forth in writing the special qualifications possessed by him which seem to them to entitle him to the honor.

CHAPTER XX.

OF HONORARY DEGREES.

119. All nominations for Honorary Degrees shall be made in writing, setting forth the full name of the nominee, his place of residence, and the name of the Trustee making the nomination.

120. The Clerk shall keep, *in retentis*, a list of nominations for Honorary Degrees that lie over, with the date of the nomination, and the name of the person making the nomination, and also the Report of the Committee on Honorary Degrees when such report shall have been made. The names of persons upon whom Degrees are not conferred within one year after the report of the Committee on Honorary Degrees upon them, shall be dropped from the Clerk's list.

121. Honorary Degrees may be voted upon at any stated meeting of the Board by ballot, but no such degree shall be conferred save at Commencement and Commemoration day and when

the candidate is present to receive it, nor shall any degree be then conferred unless it be accompanied with a public statement of the reasons for which it is given.

122. No Honorary Degree shall be bestowed on any one not recommended by the Committee on Honorary Degrees, except by a three-fourths vote of all the members of the Board.

123. The Degrees of LL.D., D.D., D.S. and Ph.D. shall not be conferred at the stated meeting at which the nomination of the candidate is made, save by the unanimous vote of the members present, in number not less then a majority of the entire Board; at the following stated meeting, however, such Degrees may be conferred by the affirmative votes of a majority of the entire Board of Trustees, in the case of one recommended by the Committee on Honorary Degrees; or, in the case of one not so recommended, by a three-fourths vote of the entire Board.

CHAPTER XXI.

OF ACADEMIC COSTUME.

124. The following academic costume is permitted to be worn by members of the Board of Trustees and of the Faculty and by other Officers and the Alumni of the University, upon all appropriate University occasions, such as the public exercises of Commemoration day, of Commencement week and whenever they appear officially in public.

GOWNS. 1. Pattern. Those commonly worn, with pointed sleeves for the Bachelor's Degree, with long, closed sleeves for the Master's Degree, and with round, open sleeves for the Doctor's Degree. 2. Material. Worsted stuff for the Bachelor's Degree, silk for the Master's and Doctor's Degrees. 3. Color. Black. 4. Trimmings. For the Bachelor's and Master's Degrees the gowns are to be untrimmed. For the Doctor's Degree the gown is to be faced down the front with black velvet, with bars of the same across the sleeves; or the facings and crossbars may be of velvet of the same color as the binding or edging of the hood, being distinctive of the Faculty to which the Degree pertains.

Hoods. 1. Pattern. The pattern usually followed by Colleges and Universities, save as modified below. 2. Material. The same as that of the gown. 3. Color. Black. 4. Length. The length and form of the hood shall indicate the Degree as follows: For the Bachelor's Degree, the length shall be three-fourths that of the Master's Degree. The hood for the Master's Degree shall be of the customary length, not exceeding four feet; and that of the Doctor's Degree shall be of the same length but have panels at the sides. 5. Linings. The hoods shall be lined with the official colors of Princeton—orange and black. 6. Trimmings. The binding or edging, not more than six inches in width, to be of silk, satin or velvet, the color to be distinctive of the Faculty to which the Degree pertains, thus: Faculty of Arts and Letters, white. Faculty of Theology, scarlet. Faculty of Law, purple. Faculty of Medicine, green. Faculty of Philosophy, dark blue. Faculty of Science, gold yellow. Faculty of Fine Arts, brown. Faculty of Music, pink.

Caps. The caps shall be of the material and form generally used, and commonly called mortar-board caps. The color shall be black. The Doctor's cap may be of velvet. Each cap shall be ornamented with a long tassel attached to the middle point at the top. The tassel of the Doctor's cap may be, in whole or in part, of gold thread.

Members of the Governing Body of the University shall be entitled, during their term of office, to wear the gown of highest dignity—that of the Doctor's Degree—together with the hood appropriate to the Degree which they may have severally received. Members of the Faculties, and any person officially connected with the University who have been recipients of academic honors from other universities or colleges in good standing, may assume the academic costume corresponding to their Degree, as described in the foregoing section, *provided*, that such right shall terminate if such persons shall cease to be connected with the University. The President and the Dean of the Faculty may adopt distinctive badges, not inconsistent with the costume hereinbefore described.

CHAPTER XXII.

OF THE ORDER OF BUSINESS.

125. A printed docket shall be placed before the Board by the Clerk at each stated meeting. The general schedule shall be as follows:

 I. Organization with Prayer.
 II. Reading of the Clerk's Certificate.
 III. Reading, correction, and approval of Minutes.
 IV. Clerk's Report.
 V. President's Report, to be referred to the Standing Committees.
 VI. Reception of Committee from the Faculty.
 VII. Presentation of Faculty Minutes and reference to Committees on the Curriculum and on Morals and Discipline.
 VIII. Nominations for Honorary Degrees.
 IX. Reports of Committees:
  1. Finance.
  2. Grounds and Buildings.
  3. Library and Apparatus.
  4. The Curriculum.
  5. Morals and Discipline.
  6. Honorary Degrees.
  7. Special Committees.
 X. Miscellaneous Business.
 XI. Balloting on Nominees for Honorary Degrees.
 XII. Special reports of the Standing Committees on the President's Report.
 XIII. Report of Committee on Morals and Discipline on Dean's Report.
 XIV. Report on Faculty Minutes.
 XV. Appointment of next meeting.
 XVI. Adjournment with prayer.

126. Other matters may be placed upon the docket as they arise, or by special order of the Board.

127. The order of business prescribed in the docket shall not be departed from, unless by a vote of the Board upon motion.

128. Whenever a matter requiring the action of a Committee shall arise, it shall be referred to the Standing Committee having charge of the subject, unless by special order of the Board.

129. Committees shall, in all cases, report to the Board in writing. Should a Standing Committee fail thus to report, such failure shall be entered in the record book of the Committee, with the reasons thereof.

130. Those entrusted with the awarding of fellowships and prizes shall report to the Board, through the Treasurer, on the first day of the meeting, except in cases where the competition takes place during the session of the Board.

CHAPTER XXIII.

MISCELLANEOUS.

131. No resolution shall be considered by the Board, unless it be first put in writing and delivered to the Clerk.

132. No change in these By-Laws shall be made, save by a vote of two-thirds of the entire Board at the stated meeting at which the proposed change is made, or by a majority vote of the members present at a stated meeting subsequent to a meeting at which notice of proposal to change such By-Law shall have been given; and no change shall be made in Chap. XX., Art. 126, at a meeting at which a change is proposed, save by a unanimous vote of the members present, in number not less than a majority of the entire Board. The operation of these By-Laws shall not be changed or suspended save by the unanimous vote of the members present, in numbers not less than a majority of the entire Board.

133. All resolutions of the Board, inconsistent with these By-Laws, are hereby repealed.

134. The actual traveling expenses of Trustees attending meetings of the Board and Committees shall be refunded to them on application to the Treasurer.

135. All proceedings of the Board, the debates, and every part of the business transacted at its meetings, shall be considered as confidential, and shall not be divulged, except officially or when permitted by the Board.

136. The Commencement Arrangements shall be under the direction of a Committee of the Board of Trustees, who shall be authorized to add to their number from the Faculty or otherwise.

Rules of Order.

Rules of Order

OF THE BOARD OF TRUSTEES.

1. The Presiding Officer shall take the chair precisely at the hour to which the Board stands adjourned ; and shall immediately call the members to order ; and, on the appearance of a quorum, shall open the session with prayer.

2. The business shall be taken up and disposed of in the order prescribed in the By-Laws.

3. The Presiding Officer may speak to points of order, in preference to other members, rising from his seat for that purpose ; and shall decide questions of order, subject to an appeal to the Board by any two members.

4. If the Presiding Officer desires to discuss any question he shall leave the chair for that purpose, and shall call the senior member of the Board present to take the chair.

5. When a vote is taken by ballot, the Presiding Officer shall vote with the other members ; but he shall not vote in any other case, unless the vote be equally divided ; when, if he do not choose to vote, the question shall be lost.

6. A motion made must be seconded, and afterwards repeated by the Presiding Officer or read aloud, before it is debated.

7. Any member who shall have made a motion, shall have liberty to withdraw it, with the consent of his second, before any debate has taken place thereon ; but not afterwards, without the leave of the Board.

8. If a motion under debate contains several parts, any member may have it divided, and a question taken on each part.

9. When various motions are made, with respect to the filling of blanks with particular numbers or times, the questions shall always be first taken on the highest number and the longest time.

10. Motions to lay on the table, to take up business, to adjourn, and the call for the previous question, shall be put without debate. On questions of order, postponement, or commitment, no member shall speak more than once; on all other questions each member may speak twice, but not oftener without express leave of the Board.

11. When a question is under debate, no motion shall be received, unless to adjourn, to lay on the table, to postpone indefinitely, to postpone to a day certain, to commit, or to amend ; which several motions shall have precedence in the order in which they are herein arranged ; and the motion of adjournment shall always be in order.

12. An amendment, and also an amendment to an amendment, may be moved on any motion ; but a motion to amend an amendment to an amendment shall not be in order. Action on amendments shall precede action on the original motion.

13. A distinction shall be observed between a motion to lay on the table for the present, and a motion to lay on the table unconditionally, viz. : A motion to lay on the table for the present shall be taken without debate ; and, if carried in the affirmative, the effect shall be to place the subject on the docket, and it may be taken up and considered at any subsequent time. But a motion to lay on the table unconditionally, shall be taken without debate ; and, if carried in the affirmative, it shall not be in order to take up the subject during the same meeting of the Board without a vote of reconsideration.

14. The previous question shall be put in this form, namely : "Shall the main question be now put ?" It shall be admitted only when demanded by a majority of the members present, and the effect shall be to put an end to all debate and bring the body to a direct vote—first, on the motion to commit the subject under consideration (if such motion shall have been made) ; secondly, if

the motion for commitment does not prevail, on pending amendments; and, lastly, on the main question.

15. A question shall not be again called up or considered at the same meeting of the Board at which it has been decided, unless by consent of two-thirds of the members who were present at the decision, and unless the motion to reconsider be made and seconded by persons who voted with the majority.

16. When the Presiding Officer has commenced taking the vote, no further debate or remarks shall be admitted, unless there has evidently been a mistake, in which case the mistake shall be rectified and the Presiding Officer shall recommence taking the vote.

17. The yeas and nays on any question shall not be recorded unless required by one-third of the members present.

18. No member, in the course of the debate, shall be allowed to indulge in personal reflections.

19. If more than one member rise to speak at the same time, the member who is most distant from the Presiding Officer's chair shall speak first.

20. When more than three members of the Board shall be standing at the same time, the Presiding Officer may require all to take their seats, the person only excepted who may be speaking.

21. Every member, when speaking, shall address himself to the Presiding Officer.

22. No speaker shall be interrupted, unless he be out of order, or for the purpose of correcting mistakes or misrepresentations.

23. Without express permission, no member of the Board, while business is going on, shall engage in private conversation.

24. Members shall attend closely, in their speeches, to the subject under consideration; and when they deviate from the subject, it shall be the privilege of any member, and the duty of the Presiding Officer, to call them to order.

25. If any member consider himself aggrieved by a decision of the Presiding Officer, it shall be his privilege to appeal to the

Board, and the question on the appeal shall be taken without debate.

26. Any member shall have the right to have his dissent from, or protest against, any action of the Board, with the reason therefor if couched in respectful language, recorded in the minutes.